A WEE BIT OF TEXAS

For Jordan Buck.
Have fun reading!
Rita Kerr
1998

By

Rita Kerr

EAKIN PRESS ★ Austin, Texas

Published in the United States of America
By Eakin Press
An Imprint of Eakin Publications, Inc.
P.O. Drawer 90159 ★ Austin, TX 78709-0159

ISBN 0-89015-809-6

Library of Congress Cataloging-in-Publication Data

Kerr, Rita.
    A wee bit of Texas / by Rita Kerr.
      p.   cm.
    Summary: While Grandfather Mouse, the smartest mouse in Texas, reads "A Wee Bit of Texas" to the mice at one of their weekly meetings, the old tom cat creeps closer and closer. Who will save the day?
    ISBN 0-89015-809-6 : $9.95
    [1. Mice — Fiction. 2. Texas — Fiction.] I. Title.
PZ7.K468458We   1991
[E] — dc20
                                            90-25015
                                                CIP
                                                AC

This book is dedicated to
the author's many little friends,
who are a wee part of Texas too.

Acknowledgments

The author wishes to thank all of the teachers and librarians who encouraged her to write this book. Special thanks goes to friends for their interest. These include "Ma" Creel, Glenda Boone, Nannette Newell, B Sharp, and many others interested in children learning about Texas.

Grandfather Mouse lived in a big house in one of
the oldest towns in Texas.

Old Grandfather Mouse was the wisest mouse in all of Texas. And no wonder. He lived in a neat little home behind some of the best books in Texas! The books were in the library of a big house located in one of the oldest towns in Texas.

Grandfather was not only wise, he was smart. He could read!

Grandfather Mouse would sit in his rocking chair
and read his books.

He was not the only mouse that lived in the big house. There were big mice and little mice. Each evening after the house became quiet, they would run this way and that, having fun. All but Grand-father. While the other mice played, he would sit in his rocking chair and read his books.

Grandfather Mouse lived on the top shelf in the
library.

Every month the mice that lived in the big house met at Grandfather Mouse's on the top shelf in the library. Fat mice and skinny mice would hurry up a rope which led to Grandfather's house. When they were all safe inside, the mice would pull up the rope and have their meeting.

At each meeting they talked about the old gray tomcat. That cat was their bitter enemy. He made their life miserable.

That cat made their life miserable.

The mice never knew where
the cat might be. He never made a
sound. He was quiet as a mouse!

Old Tom seemed to be every-
where. If the mice were in the
kitchen, the cat was there. If the
mice were in the cellar, the cat was
there. The mice learned that the
old cat was not only quiet — he was
fast!

Grandfather Mouse and Teeny were Silly-Willy's
friends.

Teeny and Sam and all of the other mice were afraid of old Tom. Even Silly-Willy was afraid. And Silly-Willy was afraid of nothing! That mouse was so silly he tied a bow on his tail and put one on Teeny's ear. Teeny was his best friend. Silly-Willy even tied a bow around Grandfather's neck.

Silly-Willy would do anything for attention!

Silly-Willy would do anything for attention. He would dance around acting silly or he would try to stand on his head. Sometimes he crossed his eyes and waved his arms to show what he could do.

Silly-Willy had many friends, but they did not think he was funny. Grandfather Mouse did not think he was funny either. He was always talking when he should have been listening!

Silly-Willy watched the other mice run up the rope
to Grandfather's house.

One night Silly-Willy and Teeny climbed the rope to Grandfather's house. They watched the other mice run up the rope. But somehow, in the excitement, they forgot to pull up the rope behind them. That was a big mistake!

"Grandfather," Teeny said, "we always talk about the cat. Tonight would you read to us from one of your fine books?"

"Oh, yes," the others cried. "Do read to us. Please, Grandfather!"

A Wee Bit of Texas

Silly-Willy tried to stand on his head.

Grandfather Mouse smiled and took one of the books from the library shelf. "Very well," he said. "It is time you learned something about Texas. I will read to you from *A Wee Bit of Texas*. Sam, will you and Squeaky turn the pages?"

"Oh, yes," Squeaky squeaked.

"Ugh! Who wants to hear that book?" Silly-Willy cried and tried to stand on his head.

"We do!" Teeny and the others said. "Sit down!"

Grandfather wrinkled his nose. He did hope Silly-Willy would sit down and listen.

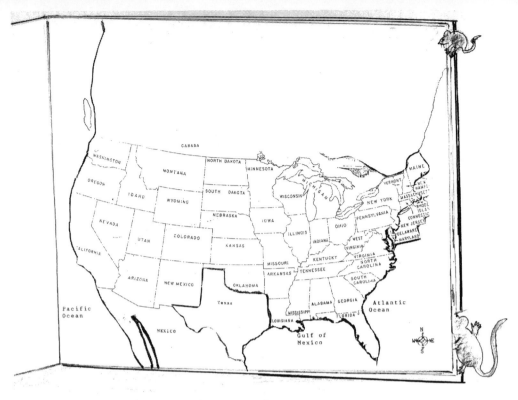

"This is a map of the United States,"
Grandfather said.

Sam and Squeaky opened the book. The others moved where they could see the pictures. Grandfather slid his glasses over his nose. "This is a map of the United States," he said, pointing to the left. "That is the Pacific Ocean. On the other side is the Atlantic Ocean. The Gulf of Mexico is at the bottom of the map."

"And there's Texas, and we live in Texas!" Silly-Willy cried.

Grandfather explained the compass.

"What's that?" Teeny asked, pointing to the corner of the page.

Grandfather smiled. "That is a compass. The N points to the north. The S points south. The W points west, and the E points east."

"North is up and south is down," Silly-Willy cried.

"*Sh-h,*" Teeny scolded. "Grandfather is going to read to us."

ɔened the book.
e they could see
father slid his
and began to
exas.

first people in
ɪdians lived in
ɪd logs. Other
-like houses
ɪans thought
m.

Some Indians lived in tent-like houses called tepees.
Others lived in houses made of grass and logs.

Grandfather nodded and began to read from the book, *A Wee Bit of Texas.*

"Indians were the first people in Texas. Some of the Indians lived in houses made of grass and logs. Other Indians lived in tent-like houses called tepees. The Indians thought Texas belonged to them," Grandfather read.

Texas was part of
...imed both Mexico and

...e claimed a small
...ch of the land was a
...were coyotes and

...illy-Willy screamed.

The flags of Spain and France were the first flags
to fly over Texas.

"At that time Texas was part of Mexico. Spain claimed both Mexico and Texas. Later, France claimed a small part of Texas. Much of the land was a wilderness.

"Texas had some strange animals, like the jack rabbit. Another strange animal of Texas was the armadillo. And the rattle-snake was another. These animals can still be found in parts of Texas.

"There were other animals in Texas, like coyotes and wild-cats. . ."

"Wild cats?" Silly-Willy screamed. "What's that?"

ed his nose. "I
ike the old Tom
wilder."
whispered. The
eir eyes.
t on reading.
nd wild cats, and buf-
Indians of
vs and arrows.
clothing from

The Indians hunted for buffalo.

Grandfather rubbed his nose. "I guess wildcats are like the old tomcat — but bigger and wilder."

"Oh!" Silly-Willy whispered. The other mice rolled their eyes.

Grandfather went on reading. "There were coyotes and wildcats, and bears, and buffalo. The Indians of Texas hunted with bows and arrows. They made tents and clothing from the buffalo skins."

The Alamo

The Indians helped build a church called the
Alamo.

"Clothes of buffalo skins? Ugh!" Silly-Willy cried, wrinkling his nose.

"*Sh-h,*" the others scolded.

Grandfather's whiskers wiggled, but he went on reading. "Spain sent priests to Texas to teach the Indians about God. The Indians helped the priests make a church in San Antonio. They called that church the Alamo.

"The Indians were happy with their new life at first. But, in time, they went back to their old ways.

freedom from
co went up over

gs!" Teeny

ndfather
turned the
n reading.
t the first
d States. He is
r of Texas'. . ."
fell open.
as?"

The flag of Mexico was the third flag to fly over
Texas.

"When Mexico won its freedom from Spain, the flag of Mexico went up over Texas."

"That makes three flags!" Teeny whispered.

"You are right," Grandfather said. Sam and Squeaky turned the page. Grandfather went on reading. "Stephen F. Austin brought the first settlers from the United States. He is often called the 'Father of Texas' . . ."

Silly-Willy's mouth fell open. "The father of *all* of Texas?"

tin brought the first
..y whispered.
..thers scolded.
..r twitched his nose and
..ny of the settlers came
..ons. It was a long,
..settlers claimed land
..egan cutting trees to
..ns. There were many

..e been the wild cats,"
..gled.

Many settlers came to Texas in covered wagons.

"Yes, Austin brought the first settlers," Teeny whispered.

"*Sh-h*," the others scolded.

Grandfather twitched his nose and went on. "Many of the settlers came in covered wagons. It was a long, hard trip. The settlers claimed land in Texas and began cutting trees to build log cabins. There were many dangers . . ."

"Must have been the wildcats," Silly-Willy giggled.

"*Sh-h!*"

imals, snakes,
s hard. The men
rees to plow the
od. The girls
nd wash and
. They had
. . ."

Teeny scolded.
d as Sam turned the
resident was
he settlers were
v laws. They
hat made Santa
alked of war."

Life was hard in early Texas.

"They faced wild animals, snakes, and Indians. Life was hard. The men and boys cleared the trees to plow the land. They hunted for food. The girls learned to make soap and wash and iron and cook and sew. They had little time for play . . ."

"Shucks!"

"*Sh-h!* Be quiet!" Teeny scolded.

Grandfather smiled as Sam turned the page. "Mexico's new president was General Santa Anna. The settlers were not happy with his new laws. They talked of freedom. That made Santa Anna very angry. He talked of war."

fight?" Silly-Willy
tting good!"
 rolled their eyes
ads.
iam B. Travis rode to
ne men to wait for
. On February 23,
 began. Colonel
ans were very brave,
rmy was too big.
36, the Alamo fell.
ans died for Texas.

On March 6, 1836, the Alamo fell.

"War? A real fight?" Silly-Willy cried. "This is getting good!"

The other mice rolled their eyes and shook their heads.

"Colonel William B. Travis rode to the Alamo with some men to wait for Santa Anna's army. On February 23, 1836, the fighting began. Colonel Travis and the Texans were very brave, but Santa Anna's army was too big.

"On March 6, 1836, the Alamo fell. Travis and his Texans died for Texas."

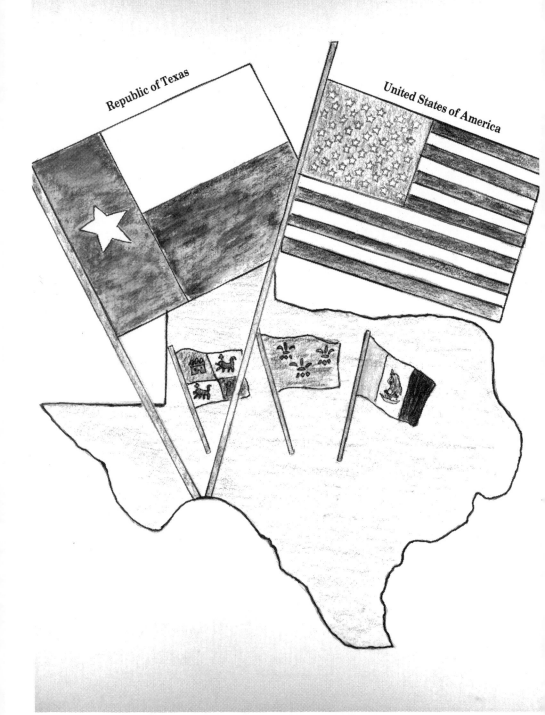

The next two flags to fly over Texas were the
flag of the Republic of Texas and the U.S. flag.

Grandfather Mouse continued. "Texas won its freedom from Mexico at the Battle of San Jacinto. The fourth flag — the Republic of Texas — went up over Texas.

"Some years later, Texas became a state of the United States. Settlers came to Texas from Europe."

"Maybe they wanted to be Texans too!" Silly-Willy giggled.

"People came from Europe on sailing ships,"
Grandfather said.

"*Sh-h,*" Teeny whispered.

But Silly-Willy wouldn't be quiet. "Did those people come in covered wagons too?"

Grandfather shook his head. "The people came from Europe on sailing ships. The trip across the Atlantic Ocean was not easy. The ships were slow. Many of the people got sick. They were happy to get to Texas."

Silly-Willy grinned a silly grin. "I told you they wanted to be Texans!"

of his whiskers
n. "The settlers
e Indians. The
eir cabins and took
iorses. They formed'
to protect . . ."
at's what we need to
at cat!" Silly-Willy

y scolded.

The Indians burned many cabins.

With a twitch of his whiskers Grandfather continued. "The settlers were afraid of the Indians. The Indians burned their cabins and took their cattle and horses. The settlers formed the Texas Rangers to protect . . ."

"Say, maybe that's what we need to protect us from that cat!" Silly-Willy screamed.

"*Sh-h!*" Teeny scolded.

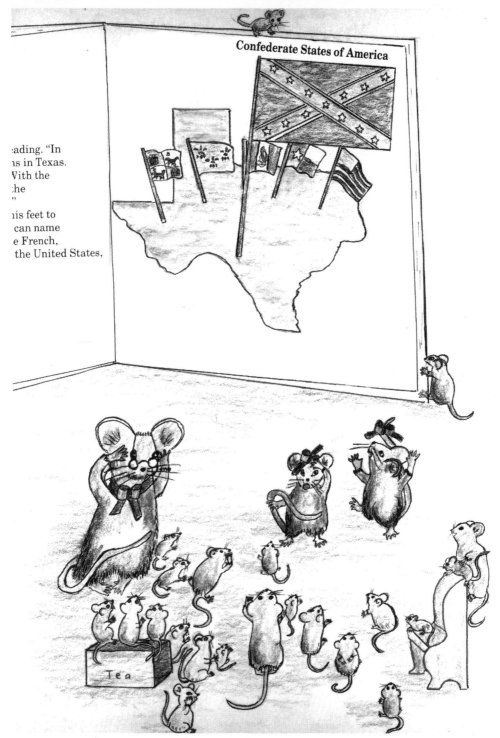

eading. "In
s in Texas.
Vith the
the
"

is feet to
can name
e French,
the United States,

The sixth flag of Texas was the Confederate flag.

Grandfather went on reading. "In time, there were more towns in Texas. New schools were opened. With the Civil War the sixth flag — the Confederate flag — went up."

Silly-Willy jumped to his feet to dance around excitedly. "I can name the flags — the Spanish, the French, the Mexican, the Republic, the United States, and . . . and . . ."

"The Confederate flag! Sit down!" Teeny squeaked.

The cowboys rounded up the longhorns to brand
them.

Grandfather again twitched his whiskers. "The Spanish had brought cows to Texas. Some of those cows wandered away and became wild. Many of those cows had long horns."

"Did they call them longhorns?" Silly-Willy asked.

Grandfather nodded and read, "After the Civil War, cowboys rounded up many of those longhorns and put their brand on them."

"You mean the cowboys put their mark on them, right?" Silly-Willy asked.

derate flag! Sit down!"
l.
istening!" Grandfather
turned the page. "By
n Texas had changed.
and airplanes . . ."
' What's that?"
vant to hear the story!"
others nodded their
ather smiled and went on

Life in Texas changed.

"You were listening!" Grandfather laughed as Sam turned the
page. "By the 1900s, life in Texas
had changed. Trains and cars and
airplanes . . ."

"Airplane? What's that?"

"Sh-h! We want to hear the
story!" Sam cried. The others nodded
their heads. Grandfather smiled as
Sam turned the page.

Grandfather pointed out some of the towns of Texas.

"Now," Grandfather said.
"This map shows some of the towns
and rivers in Texas. Three of the
largest cities are Dallas, Houston,
and San Antonio."

Silly-Willy ran to the map.
"That's San Antonio, and there's a
picture of the Alamo!"

"Yes," Grandfather said. "Who
can find Houston?"

"I can. It is right there," Teeny
cried. "What is this?"

Grandfather smiled. "That is
Austin. Austin is the capital of
Texas."

The old cat was settling down in his favorite chair.

Grandfather did not know that while he was reading, the old gray tomcat had come into the library. He had jumped into his favorite chair and was settling down for the night. The cat was almost asleep when he heard a squeak.

He opened one eye and then the other. The tomcat knew that squeak. It was the noise made by a mouse!

The cat pulled on the rope.

The cat sat up slowly and looked around the room. Then he saw the rope hanging from the top shelf — the one the mice had forgotten!

Old Tom slid from his chair and quietly moved across the floor to look at the rope. He gave it a tug. Nothing happened. He pulled again. It did not come down. The cat was sure that rope would lead him to the mouse!

Old Tom heard not just one mouse, but many mice!

Ever so quietly, the cat put one paw and then the other on the rope, just as he did when he climbed a tree. His heart beat faster as he started up the rope. He moved higher and higher. The squeaking grew louder and louder.

The cat's nose twitched with excitement. He heard not just one mouse but many mice! Old Tom's tail moved from side to side. His hair stood on end as he neared the end of the rope. He stopped and listened.

"Run for your lives! The cat is here!"

"What did you like about the book?" Grandfather was saying. All of the mice talked at once.

The old cat slowly pulled himself up the rope to peek over the shelf. He saw big mice and little mice! The cat smacked his lips and put out his paw to catch one.

At that moment Teeny screamed. "Help! It's the cat!"

"*Ee-e-k,*" the others cried. "Run for your lives! The cat is here! The cat is here!"

Silly-Willy sank his sharp teeth into the rope.

The mice ran this way and that to get away. All but Silly-Willy. He did not run.

He looked at the cat hanging on to the rope. He saw there was only one thing to do. He must cut that rope with his teeth!

Silly-Willy slid toward the rope. He felt the cat breathing down his neck as he sank his sharp teeth into the rope.

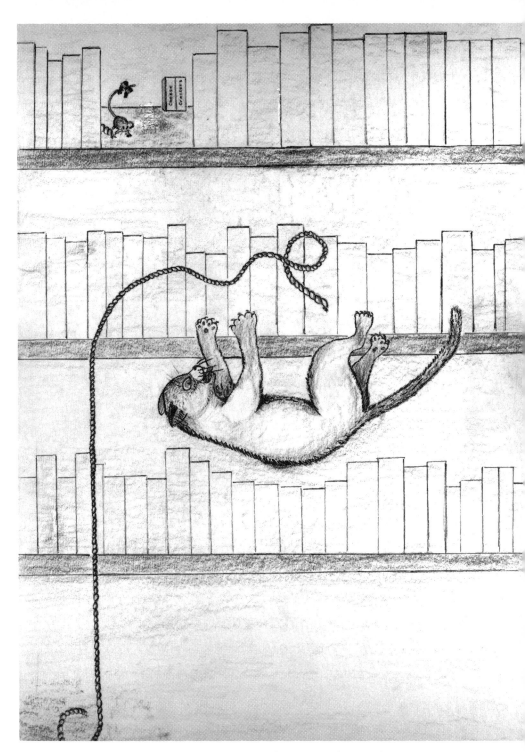

The cat found himself flying through the air!

The cat tried and tried to get his claws into Silly-Willy. He could not.

Silly-Willy worked faster and faster. He had never chewed so hard in his life. When he cut through one of the cords of the rope and then another, his heart skipped a beat. The rope grew thinner and thinner. Slowly, ever so slowly, the last cord gave way. The cat found himself flying through the air with the rope!

"E-e-e-owee!" the old cat screamed, clawing wildly as he fell. He hit the floor with a thud!

The cat walked away sad and hungry.

Silly-Willy and Grandfather watched from the shelf above.

Old Tom shook his head and stood slowly on his feet. His legs wobbled as he walked slowly across the floor. At the doorway, the old cat looked back and shook his head. He had been so near to those mice! He walked away sad and hungry.

"Come out! It's safe," Silly-Willy cried.

One by one the mice came back. "We're safe! We're safe!" Teeny cried.

"We are really safe!" the others sang happily.

Silly-Willy hung his head.

"*Sh-h,*" Teeny cried. "Grandfather is trying to speak."

All of the mice looked at Grandfather Mouse and waited for him to put the book back into place.

Grandfather Mouse began. "My friends, we all know that Silly-Willy can be silly."

All of the mice nodded their heads.

Grandfather looked from Silly-Willy to the other mice. "But why has he been silly? Could it be that he thought you would like him better if he made you laugh?"

The mice looked at Grandfather in surprise. Silly-Willy hung his head.

The mice danced around Silly-Willy.

"But I like him better when he isn't being silly," Teeny whispered softly.

"Me too," said Sam.

"Me too," Squeaky squeaked.

Silly-Willy looked surprised. He said, "You do?"

The others nodded.

Grandfather smiled. "My friends, Silly-Willy's quick thinking has saved us all. From this day he will be known as Willy. This mouse is not silly — he has a brave heart and is special!"

They all began dancing around Willy, singing, "Yea for Willy! He is special!"

Everyone clapped and cheered as Willy stood on his head.

"Speech! Speech!" Teeny cried proudly.

Willy wiggled his ears. He grinned from ear to ear as only a mouse can do. "Shucks! All of you are special. Y'all are a wee bit of Texas too!"

Everyone clapped and cheered as Willy stood on his head.

Bibliography

On Mice

Burton, Robert. *The Mouse in the Barn*. Milwaukee: Gareth Stevens Publishing, 1988.

Fischer-Nagel, Heiderose. *A Look Through the Mouse Hole*. Minneapolis: Carolrhoda Books, Inc., 1989.

Oakley, Graham. *The Church Mouse*. New York: Anteneum, 1972.

Oxford Scientific Films. *House Mouse*. New York: G. P. Putnam's Sons, 1978.

Sullivan, James A. *Whitefoot Mouse*. New York: Coward, McCann & Geoghegan, Inc., 1975.

On Texas

Baker, Amy Jo. *Texas Past to Present*. Lexington: D.C. Heath and Company, 1988.

Bollinger, Bill and Linda. *Texas: Your State's Story*. Austin: Steck-Vaughn Company, 1978.

Warren, Betsy, and Martha Ingerson. *The Story of Texas*. Ranch Gate, 1974.